Siblings in the Stars

SRA

Columbus, OH

SRAonline.com

 SRA

Send all inquiries to this address:
SRA/McGraw-Hill
4400 Easton Commons
Columbus, OH 43219

ISBN: 978-0-07-608766-2
MHID: 0-07-608766-2

1 2 3 4 5 6 7 8 9 NOR 13 12 11 10 09 08 07

The McGraw·Hill Companies

They were the bluest, clearest Florida skies that I had ever seen. A light morning breeze blew around us, and in the distance the space shuttle sat on the launch pad.

It was June 5, 1991. My papa, mama, and little sister Lucy and I had made the early-morning trip to the Kennedy Space Center to watch the shuttle launch. You could feel the excitement in the air from the gathering crowd.

"Papa, I want to be an astronaut someday," I said.

"Me too, Papa," my sister added. "I would make a better astronaut than Rico."

"You both can be astronauts," Papa said.

"I have confidence that you both can be anything you want to be," Mama said, trying to keep Lucy and me from arguing. "I'm sure of it."

A big digital clock was counting down to liftoff. We had a two-hour wait until the launch, so we set our chairs on the grass, surrounded by hundreds of other people.

"When did the first shuttle go into space?" Lucy asked.

Lucy knew you could ask Papa any question about the space shuttle and he would know the answer.

"The first space shuttle went into space in 1981," Papa answered.

"Do you remember it, Lucy?" I looked at my little sister and smiled, knowing she had not been born then. I didn't remember the first launch because I was only two years old, but I did not let her know that.

Papa told us that the first mission lasted for only two days and that there were only two astronauts on board. "Those first flights had an impact on today's missions. Now there are up to seven crew members, and they often stay in space for over a week," Papa said.

"There are so many people here!" Lucy said excitedly, gesturing across the lawn. "Some of them are waving little Mexican flags. Why are they doing that, Mama?"

"Well we haven't said anything, but there's a special reason we brought you here today," Mama said.

"Sid Gutierrez, the first Hispanic astronaut to command the shuttle, is flying today," Papa said proudly.

I was really surprised by Papa's comment. I had assumed there had been Hispanic astronauts before now.

"He's also going to be the pilot on this mission," Papa added.

Papa told us all about Gutierrez. In the Air Force Gutierrez had logged over 4,500 hours in jets, balloons, and rockets. Part of his job on this mission was to perform tests on how humans and animals respond to being weightless. Papa knew all this from reading about him in newspapers and magazines.

I was surprised to hear about all his responsibilities. He must be an important part of the trip if he had so many jobs to do.

"This is a special day, not only for us, but for our culture as well," Mama reminded us.

"I think it will be a special day when girls are astronauts," Lucy said.

"Actually there have been women astronauts for years, Lucy," Papa said. "Sally Ride was the first American woman in space. She was on the space shuttle's seventh mission, in 1983. Ellen Ochoa, a Hispanic woman, is currently training for a future shuttle mission."

"I wanted to be the first Hispanic woman in space." Lucy pouted. "Well maybe I'll be the first woman to live on the moon. I might even make a fantastic cosmic discovery!"

"That would make me very proud," Mama said.

"How about me, Papa? Would you be proud if I became an astronaut?" I asked.

"Absolutely! Your mama and I would both love to come and witness your first space shuttle launch," Papa said.

I imagined what that initial flight would be like. I imagined I was the pilot, like Sid Gutierrez. I would soar to distant planets like Venus and possibly find some aliens there. I would stay with them for a while, learn how they lived, and bring them back to Earth to live with us. And whenever they asked, I would fly them back home to their faraway planet. I smiled as I thought of it.

"If you want to be astronauts, you'll have a lot of work to do," Mama warned.

"A lot of work and thousands of hours of training," Papa added. "The astronaut training program is split into two main sections: basic training and advanced training. Each level of training takes about one year to complete. First you'll learn about science, technology, and the space shuttle system."

Papa took a deep breath and continued, "You will practice space walking in water and will fly jets. You will read all the training manuals. You will also learn about all the computer systems. And that is just *some* of the training."

"Finally if you're chosen for a mission you'll spend about ten months training for your specific job and learning all the details about how the shuttle works," Papa said.

I started thinking about how much fun all that training would be. I liked school, so I knew I would love learning to be an astronaut. I was a great swimmer and had "flown" when doing jumps on my skateboard, so I thought I would be the perfect astronaut.

"I'm so smart that they wouldn't make me do all that stuff," Lucy said.

"Sure, Lucy. They might let you fly the shuttle today if you ask," I said. We all started laughing.

It was 9:23 in the morning, and the countdown clock had only about a minute left before liftoff. I looked around me. The entire crowd was focused on the launch pad. Papa put his arm around my shoulder, and Mama and Lucy gathered next to us.

The shuttle looked beautiful—white and huge, standing straight up on the launch pad, like a tall giant waiting to leap into the sky.

"If I were on the shuttle, I would tell Mr. Gutierrez to steer it straight toward the moon," Lucy said.

"If I were there I'd tell him *buena suerte*—good luck," I said.

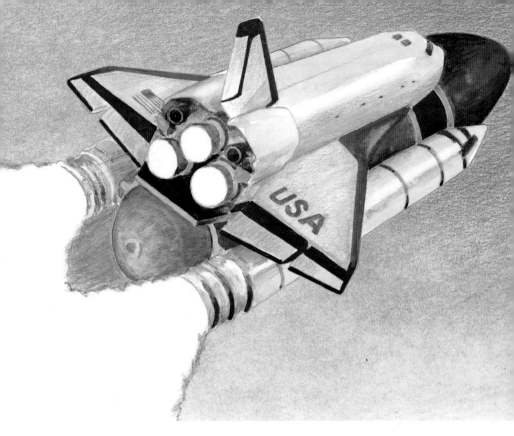

"Shh, kids, it's almost time," Mama said.

The silence broke after the countdown clock hit eleven seconds, and the crowd counted together: "10, 9, 8, 7, 6, 5, 4, 3, 2, 1, blastoff!"

The shuttle started to rumble as a huge cloud of smoke came from beneath it. That thundering rumble filled the sky, and then the machine, with an enormous thrust, shot off the launch pad. It moved slowly at first, but then it gained great speed as it rose higher into the air. We watched in amazement as it disappeared into space.

"It was truly the most dramatic day in my life, like something you see in the movies." Rico Juarez ended his story about the day his family watched the shuttle launch and looked at the students sitting in the classroom. Most of them wore the same expression he had had on his face that day many years earlier.

"I would like to thank your teacher, Ms. Gomez, for letting me come and share my story," Rico said.

The children began clapping. Ms. Gomez went to stand next to him.

"Thank you, Mr. Juarez. We are very proud of you and know that you will make an excellent astronaut," Ms. Gomez said.

A young girl raised her hand, and Ms. Gomez acknowledged her. "Megan, do you have a question for Mr. Juarez?"

"What happened to your sister Lucy? Did she become an astronaut too?" Megan asked.

"She's well on her way to becoming the famous astronaut she wanted to be. She's in her third year of college and will probably be smarter in astronomy than I am." Rico grinned.

"Do you two still tease each other?" a boy blurted out.

"Well let's put it this way: She's still my sister, so I'm hoping she'll get that home she's always wanted on the moon," Rico joked.

Vocabulary

responsibilities (ri spon´ sə bil´ i tēz) (page 7) *n.* Plural of **responsibility:** Something that is a person's job, duty, or concern.

cosmic (koz´ mik) (page 8) *adj.* Of or relating to the universe.

processes (prä´ se səz´) (page 10) *n.* Plural of **process:** A series of actions performed in making or doing something.

focused (fō´ kəst) (page 12) *v.* Past tense of **focus:** To direct attention to someone or something.

thrust (thrust) (page 13) *n.* A sudden, strong push or force.

dramatic (drə ma´ tik) (page 14) *adj.* Exciting or interesting.

Comprehension Focus: Fantasy and Reality

1. Is this book realistic fiction or a fantasy? How do you know?

2. Which parts of Rico's story are based on reality? Which parts are based on fantasy?